THIS WALKER BOOK BELONGS TO:

For Amelia and David

First published 1990 by
Walker Books Ltd, 87 Vauxhall Walk
London SE11 5HJ

This edition published 1997

10 9 8 7 6 5 4 3 2

© 1990 Patrick Benson

This book has been typeset in Garamond.

Printed in Hong Kong

British Library Cataloguing in Publication Data
A catalogue record for this book is
available from the British Library.

ISBN 0-7445-6056-X

LITTLE PENGUIN

PATRICK BENSON

WALKER BOOKS

AND SUBSIDIARIES

LONDON • BOSTON • SYDNEY

Here's Pip –
who lives in the Antarctic.
She's an Adelie penguin

and she's three years old.
Pip often goes exploring.
Here she is, walking past

some other penguins. These are Emperor penguins, who also live in the Antarctic.

Some of them are three too, but they're all much bigger than Pip.

"Why am I a little penguin?" Pip wondered, as she walked up a snow-covered hill.

"Why aren't I a big penguin?" she wondered, as she tobogganed back down.

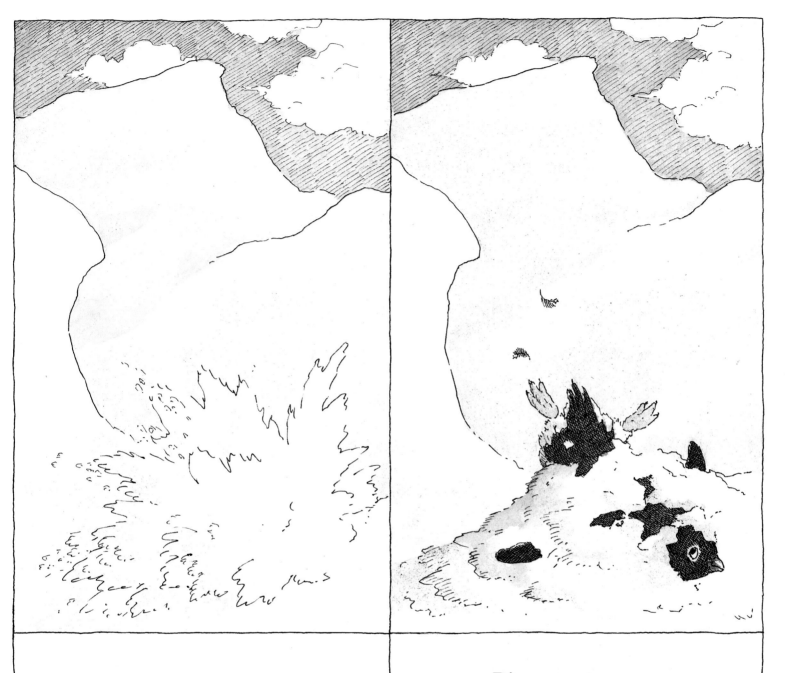

WHUMPH!

Pip went

head first into

a snow-drift.

I'm a little penguin, I am three,

sang Pip, as she skated

over the ice.

WHUMPH!

She did a somersault and landed upside down.

I'm a little penguin by the sea, sang Pip, as she came to the edge of the ice.

She jumped into the sea and landed with an enormous ...

SPLASH!

"Why are some fish little?"
wondered Pip, as she dived
deep down.

"Why are some fish big?"

she wondered, as she

shot back up.

I'm a little penguin, look at me,

sang Pip, as she swam past

something huge and black.

Pip jumped ...   on to the huge black thing.

She slipped and tumbled.

SPLASH!

I spy with my little eye, thought Pip, as she plunged

through the clear, bright water.

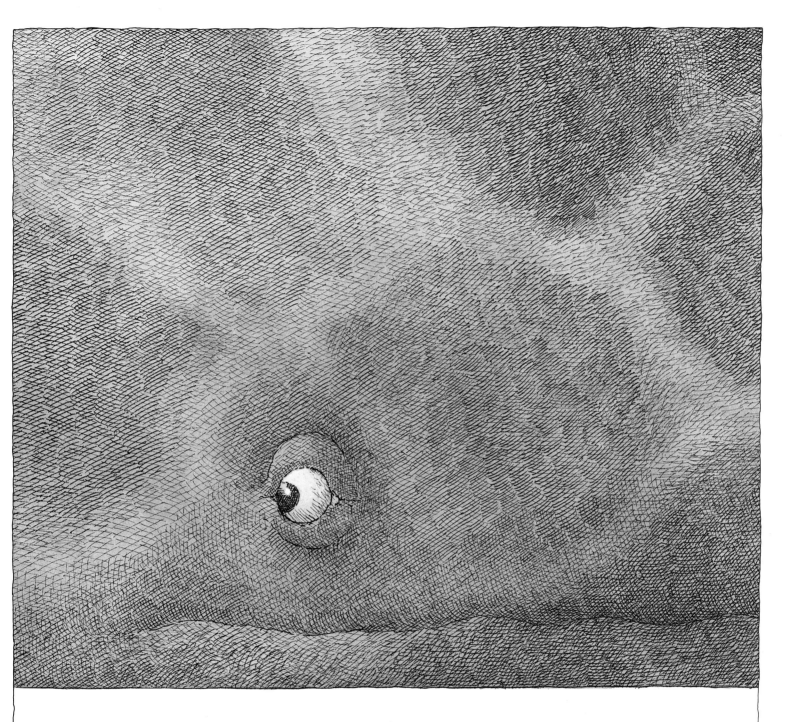

And what she spied was another eye,

spying back at her.

This is William, who visits

the Antarctic every year.

He's a Sperm whale and

he's three years old.

Pip and William played together ...

and as they played, Pip sang:

I'm a little penguin by the sea,

I love you and you love me.

One is one and two is two,

You love me and I love you.

Pip's an Adelie penguin. She lives in the Antarctic and she's three years old.

On her way home, she walks past the Emperor penguins again.

HUMPH!

They're big,

but not huge, she thinks.

That's all.